Stick Kid

Peter Holwitz

For Jesse and Cali

Published simultaneously in
canada. Manufactured in china
by South china Printing co.
Ltd. Design by Gina DiMassi.
The text is set in Bokka Solid.
The art for this book was
created with pencil, Magic
Marker and chalk on vellum.
Library of congress cataloging-in-
Publication Data   Holwitz, Peter.
Stick kid / Peter   Holwitz. p. cm.
Summary: A stick   figure boy grows
up, eventually leaving   home and starting
a stick family of his   own. [1. Growth—
Fiction. 2. Fathers and   Sons—Fiction.]
I. Title. PZ8.3.H745   St 2004 [E]—dc21
2003006089   ISBN 0-399-24163-9

1 3 5 7 9 10 8 6 4 2
First Impression

Stick Kid

Peter Holwitz

PHILOMEL BOOKS   NEW YORK

I once drew a stick kid.
Just a quick little stick kid.
I gave him two eyes
and a push-up nose.
Ten little fingers
and ten little toes.

I drew a big smile
right under his nose.
I gave him two ears
and little stick clothes.

I looked at my stick kid.
I was proud as could be. . . .

Then he opened his eyes
and looked up at me!

He said,
"I'm your stick kid.
Your quick little stick kid."

He did.

He said, "Pick me up."
He said, "Put me down."
He asked me to turn
the book upside down.

So I picked the book up.
I put the book down.
I picked the book up . . .

. . . and turned it around.

And he said,
"I'm your stick kid.
Your quick little stick kid."

That's what he said
as his face turned red.

He liked to hide
and then get found.
So I closed my eyes
and turned around.
He ran off to hide
in the back of the book.
I took my time,
but I knew where to look.

I drew him a bird,
but the bird flew away.
"I'm sorry," I said.
"Some birds don't stay."

So he asked for a monkey.
I drew the whole zoo. . . .

He asked for the moon.
I drew that too.
And I said,

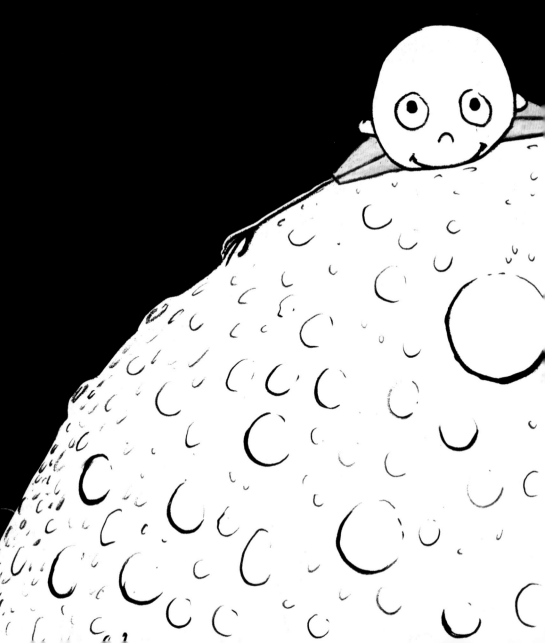

"You're my stick kid.
My sweet little stick kid."

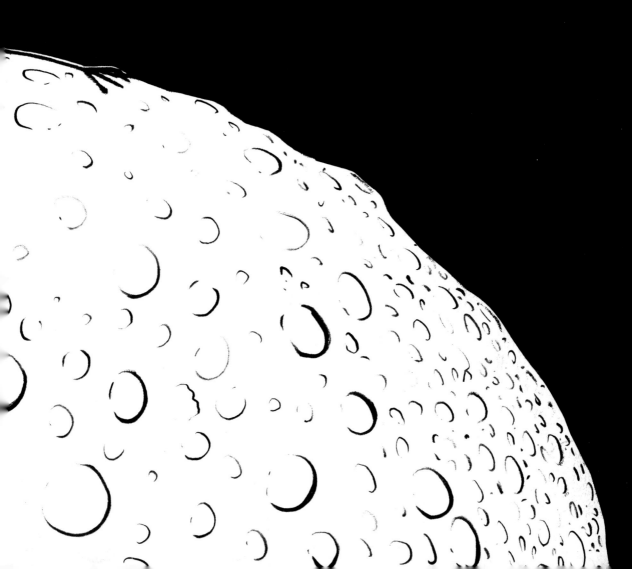

But then it got strange—
he started to change.
His ears stuck out and his legs grew long.
The clothes I drew all fit him wrong.
His eyes looked small 'cause his head just grew.
He didn't look like the kid I once drew.

And I asked,
"Would you like to climb?
I'll draw a tree!
Would you like to swim?
I'll draw the sea!"

"I want a friend," is what he said.
And I asked, "What about me?"

"No," he said. "I don't need you.
I need a friend who's a stick kid too."

So I drew a friend. I drew a few.
I drew his friends' friends,
and their friends too.

I drew the sea
and I drew the sun.
I said,
"There's my stick kid
having fun."

But he never stopped changing.
He kept rearranging.

I drew a boat
and he went fishing. . . .

I drew the stars
and he went wishing.

I drew him a bike.
He rode it far.
He asked for a road
and a little stick car.

I drew it all.
I drew it good.
I always drew the best I could.

Then one night, when day was through,
he drove away on the road I drew.

And I wondered,
Where is my stick kid?
My quick little stick kid?

Time went by.
It really flew.
I looked at the very
first picture I drew.

And I wondered,
How is my stick kid?
My quick little stick kid?

Then one day,
right out of the blue,
came a beautiful car.
It looked brand-new.

Whose car was it?
I never saw it.
And I'm pretty certain
I didn't draw it.

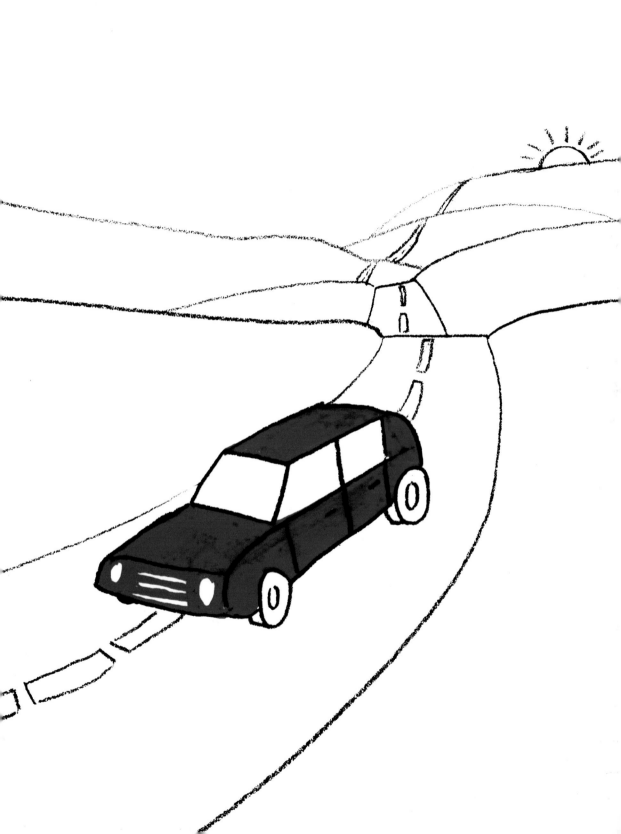

The door opened wide
and a stick man appeared.
He had a warm smile
and a well-trimmed beard.
He said,
"I'm your stick kid,
your quick little stick kid.

"But now I'm a stick man,
with a stick man's life.
This is *my* stick kid.
And my lovely stick wife."

So I smiled wide.
I told him I missed him.
I picked up the book.
I hugged them
and kissed them.

I once drew a stick kid,
and I'm happy to tell.
I once drew a stick kid,
and he grew up well.